Illustrated by John Bianchi
Written by Frank B. Edwards
Copyright 1992 by Bungalo Books

Printed in Canada for:
Bungalo Books
Box 129
Newburgh, Ontario
KOK 2S0

Co-published in U.S.A. by:
Firefly Books (U.S.) Inc.
Ellicott Station
P.O. Box 1338
Buffalo, N.Y.
14205

Trade Distribution:
Firefly Books Ltd.
250 Sparks Avenue
Willowdale, Ontario
M2H 2S4

Canadian Cataloguing in Publication Data

Edwards, Frank B., 1952
    Grandma Mooner lost her voice

ISBN 0-921285-19-1 (bound)
ISBN 0-921285-17-5 (pbk.)

I. Bianchi, John   II. Title.

PS8559.D845G73 1992 jc813'.54   C92-090404-1
PZ7.E49Gr. 1992

Bungalo Books

GRANDMA MOONER

LOST HER VOICE!

By John Bianchi & Frank B. Edwards

It was Sunday, and Melody and
Mortimer were ready for a visit from
Grandma Mooner.

"Bad news," said Mother Mooner.
"Grandma has lost her voice and can't
come over today."
"That's awful," cried Mortimer.
"I think we had better go find it," said
Melody.

RING!

First, they went to the hockey rink. Grandma Mooner never missed the Pokeweed Pucksters weekend games. They looked under the seats. And behind the penalty box. And on top of the scoreboard. There was no voice, but Mortimer found a broken hockey stick and a puck.

"How will she read us stories?" asked Melody.

"How will she call us for lunch?" worried Mortimer.

"We had better keep looking," they both agreed.

They went to the Opera House.
Grandma Mooner loved to sing the
maiden's lament in *El Pigaroni*.
  They looked under the stage. And
behind the curtain. And on top of the
balcony. There was no voice, but
Melody found some broken opera
glasses and a crumpled hanky.

"How will she sing us to sleep?"
asked Melody.

"How will she order popcorn at the
movies?" worried Mortimer.

"We had better keep looking," they
both agreed.

They went to the health club. Grandma Mooner had recently bounced her way to the county aerobic championships.
They looked in the lockers. And behind the water cooler. And under the exercise mats. There was no voice, but Mortimer found two shoelaces and a polka–dot headband.

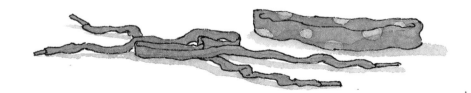

"How will she phone
us after school?"
asked Melody.

"How will she choose doughnuts for us at the bakery?" worried Mortimer.
"We had better keep looking," they both agreed.

They went to the wrestling arena. Grandma Mooner had once received autographs from both The Gruesome Twosome Twins.

They looked under the canvas. And behind the ticket counter. And on top of the bell. There was no voice, but Melody found The Red Marauder's mask and a battered umbrella.

"How will she cheer for us at baseball?" asked Melody.

"How will she ask who wants dessert?" worried Mortimer.

"We had better keep looking," they both agreed.

Melody and Mortimer trudged all over town, looking for Grandma Mooner's voice in all of her favourite places. They searched the mall, the town square, the library, the auction barn and even the arcade.

And although they found a wagonful of great stuff, they could not find Grandma Mooner's voice anywhere.

"We had better go tell her we couldn't find it," said Melody.

"Maybe she left it in her refrigerator," said Mortimer hopefully.

When they arrived at Grandma Mooner's house, she was waiting for them at the front door.

"How are you, my little darlings?" she croaked softly.

"You can still talk," shouted Melody.

"You didn't lose your voice after all," sighed Mortimer.

"No, not really," laughed Grandma Mooner...

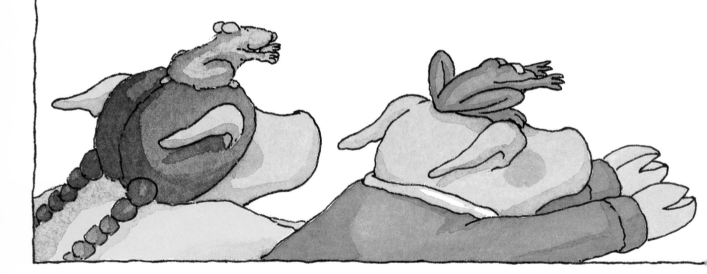

This Bungalo Book Was Brought to You by...

John Bianchi, a cartoonist, illustrator and author who lives near Bath, Ontario, with his family. His work has appeared frequently in *Harrowsmith* magazine and many other periodicals. John has more than a dozen children's books to his credit and travels across North America conducting writing and illustration workshops.

Frank B. Edwards, a former feature writer and editor with *Equinox* and *Harrowsmith* magazines. He lives with his family in Newburgh, a small eastern Ontario village. Frank and John have been editorial collaborators since 1985, the year they founded Bungalo Books, the world's most fun-loving book-publishing company.

Official Bungalo Reading Buddies

Kids who love to read books are eligible to become official, card–carrying Bungalo Reading Buddies. If you and your friends want to join an international club dedicated to having fun while reading, show this notice to your teacher or librarian. We'll send your class a great membership kit. Everyone can become a member.

Teachers and Librarians

Bungalo Books would be pleased to send you a Reading Buddy membership kit that includes 25 full-colour, laminated membership cards. These pocket-sized, 2¼-by-4-inch membership cards can be incorporated into a wide variety of school and community reading programmes for primary, junior and intermediate elementary school students.

✳ **Each kit includes 25 membership cards, a current Bungalo Reading Buddy newsletter, and an autographed Bungalo Boys adventure book.**

✳ **Kits cost only $7.50 for postage and handling.**

✳ **No cash please. Make cheque or money order payable to Bungalo Books.**

✳ **Offer limited to libraries and schools.**

✳ **Please allow two weeks for delivery.**

Bungalo World Headquarters
Box 129
Newburgh, Ontario
K0K 2S0